LEGENDS
-OF THE-
STARS

THIS IS A CARLTON BOOK

Published in 2019 by Carlton Books Limited,
an imprint of the Carlton Publishing Group,
20 Mortimer Street, London W1T 3JW

A catalogue record for this book is available from the British Library.

Design: Advantage London
Managing Art Editor: Matt Drew
Editor: Jenni Lazell
Production: Nicola Davey

10 9 8 7 6 5 4 3 2 1

ISBN: 978-1-78312-490-9

Printed in China

Picture Acknowledgements

The publisher would like to thank the following sources for their kind permission to reproduce the pictures in this book.
t = top; l = left; c = centre; r = right; b = bottom

Pages 1–5, 24–25 b/g, 54–55 b/g, 60–61 b/g, 70–72 Skylines/Shutterstock; 6–7 yoshi0511/Shutterstock; 8–9 b/g Yeloo/Shutterstock; 8c Wellcome Library, London/Wikicommons; 9 Wang Zhiyuan & Huan Shang/Wikicommons; 9t, 46 bilwissedition Ltd. & Co. KG/Alamy; 9c Dja65/Shutterstock; 9b, 10 Science History Images/Alamy; 10–11 b/g suparerk karuehanon/Shutterstock; 11br vcahi/Shutterstock; 11t ployy/Shutterstock; 12–13 b/g, 38-39 b/g Andy Holmes/Unsplash; 12–13 satiago silver/Adobe stock; 12 AnNinniah/Shutterstock; 14–15 Denis Belitsky/Shutterstock; 16–17, 46-47 b/g Vadim Sadovski/Shutterstock; 16 Christos Georghiou/Shutterstock; 16r, 19r, 55b NASA; 17br Wolfgang Sauber/Wikicommons; 18–19 b/g del Monaco/Shutterstock; 18–19 grapeot/Shutterstock; 18 Holger Kirk/Shutterstock; 19l pict rider/Adobe stock; 20–21 b/g, 26–27 b/g, 62–63 b/g Igor Kovalchuk/Shutterstock; 20–21b Vibe Images/Shutterstock; 22–23 b/g, 30-31 b/g, 32–33 b/g ANON MUEMPROM/Shutterstock; 22–23 Sergey Uryadnikov/Shutterstock; 22 Frank Kirchback/Wikicommons; 23 Ramanarayanadatta astri/Wikicommons; 24l Catalin Petolea/Shutterstock; 26–27 Laszlo86/Shutterstock; 26b Rostslav Stach/Shutterstock; 27b Mountains Hunter/Shutterstock; 28–29 b/g pixelparticle/Shutterstock; 28–29 tony mills/Shutterstock; 28 The Granger Collection/Alamy; 29 Paolo Gallo/Shutterstock; 30–31 Vlanetyna Chukhlyebova/Shutterstock; 30 Ivy Close Images/Alamy; 31b Rama/Wikicommons; 31t Nataly Studio/Shutterstock; 32 Princeton University Art Museum; 33 Tragoolchitr Jittasaiyapan/Shutterstock; 34–35 b/g Milosz_G/Shutterstock; 34–35 Antero Topp/Shutterstock; 34 Artokoloro Quint Lox Limited/Alamy; 35 RODKARV/Shutterstock; 36-37 b/g Hitdelight/Shutterstock; 36–37 Dennis W Donohue/Shutterstock; 36 Peter Wey/Shutterstock, Tyler Olson/Shutterstock, Cattallina/Shutterstock, Rober Adrien Hillman/Shutterstock; 37 RelentlessImages/Shutterstock; 38–39 tusneomp/Shutterstock; 40–41 b/g, 48–49 b/g Igor Peftiev/Unsplash; 42–43 b/g, 43 steve/Adobe stock; 42l Eric Isselee/Shutterstock; 42 storm/Adobe stock; 44–45 Michal Macnewicz/Unsplash; 44–45 Bettmann/Getty Images; 44 Carole Raddato/Flickr; 45 Jurik Peter/Shutterstock; 46–47 RGB Ventures/Superstock/Alamy; 47 menierd/Shutterstock; 50–51 b/g TitleWatsa/Shutterstock; 50–51 Classic Image/Alamy; 50 Painters/Alamy; 51 Belish/Shutterstock; 52 Alfredo Dagli Orti/REX/Shutterstock; 53t Anatoly Vartanov/Shutterstock; 54 BasPhoto/Shutterstock; 55t Artur Balytskyi/Shutterstock; 56–57 b/g Stocktrek Images, Inc./Alamy; 58–59 b/g Alan Dyer/VWPics/Alamy; 58–59 Benny Marty/Alamy; 59bl Asar Studios/Alamy; 59b Renato P Castilho/Shutterstock; 60 MattLphotography/Shutterstock; 60–61 b/g brulove/Shutterstock; 60–61 AlgolOnline/Alamy; 64–65 b/g Genevieve de Messieres/Shutterstock; 64 World History Archive/Alamy; 65 North Wind Picture Archives/Alamy; 66–67 b/g Rovsky/Shutterstock; 66b Peter Horree/Alamy; 66 koya979/Shutterstock; 67b Stocktrek Images, Inc.,/Alamy; 68–69 b/g Josip Ninkovic/Shutterstock; 68-69 serkan mutan/Shutterstock, Rafal Szozda/Shutterstock; 68 Pictures Now/Alamy; 69 KGP_Payless/Shutterstock.

LEGENDS -OF THE- STARS

CARLTON
KIDS

MYTHS OF THE NIGHT SKY

Stella Caldwell

CONTENTS

INTRODUCTION

*A*cross the centuries, people from every part of the world have gazed up at the sparkling night sky and seen patterns and pictures hiding amongst the stars.

Our ancestors lived much closer to nature than we do today—they spent more time outside and there was no artificial light to distract them. Observing the movement of the sun, moon, and stars was vital for timekeeping and navigation: people were able to predict the changing seasons and know when to plant crops, while ancient travelers used the stars to guide them on long journeys.

It is not surprising that people connected the stars into recognizable patterns, and great heroes, powerful gods, and fearsome beasts all took their place in the heavens. These myths and legends from around the world provide a direct link to our ancestors. And although great strides in science mean that we understand a lot more about our place in the universe—and what the stars, moon, and planets actually are—we can still feel the same sense of wonder and magic when we gaze up at the night sky and see the same patterns.

ANCIENT SKIES

For our ancestors, stargazing was of great importance. The discoveries made by ancient Greek astronomers, such as Ptolemy and Aristotle, paved the way for later scientists. We owe much of our current knowledge of the stars and planets to the passion of these early astronomers for uncovering the mysteries of the night sky.

A Chinese painting of Ursa Major

THE CONSTELLATIONS

Across the ages, many different cultures have seen patterns in the stars, grouping them together as "constellations." Since many of these overlapped, in 1930 scientists created an official star map consisting of 88 constellations to cover the entire night sky. Forty-eight of these were named by the ancient Greeks around 2,000 years ago. The remainder were introduced in the sixteenth and seventeenth centuries when astronomers made new discoveries and explorers ventured to the southern hemisphere.

Although the sky above us seems permanent, the universe is constantly shifting. Scientists predict that in 50,000 years' time, many of the major constellations will be unrecognizable.

"...When I follow at my pleasure the multitude of the stars in their circular course, my feet no longer touch the Earth."
Claudius Ptolemy, second century AD

THE ALMAGEST

In the second century AD, the Greek astronomer Claudius Ptolemy published his great treatise on the motions of the stars and planets, the *Almagest*. Basing the work on historical data as well as his own observations, Ptolemy named many of the constellations that are familiar to us today. The *Almagest* remained the basic textbook on western astronomy until the eighteenth century.

***Below: Page from the* Almagest**

THE
CELESTIAL SPHERE

In ancient times, many people believed that Earth was surrounded by a giant rotating dome embedded with stars. Of course, we now know this is incorrect, but astronomers still use the "celestial sphere" model to describe the positions and motions of the stars.

IMAGINARY SPHERE

Even though the stars all appear to have the same distance from Earth, they are scattered throughout the Milky Way. However, the idea of a sphere, with stars fixed to the inside of it, allows astronomers to give the stars a position on a star map. Like Earth, the celestial sphere has north and south poles, aligned with Earth's poles, and a celestial equator, lying above Earth's equator. At any one time, a person gazing up at the sky can only see one side of the celestial sphere—the other half lies below the horizon.

Celestial sphere model—1521

MOVING STARS

Over the course of a night, the stars seem to rise in the east and set in the west, tracing an arc as they move across the sky. This is because Earth is spinning on its axis. In the northern hemisphere, the stars appear to circle counterclockwise around the north celestial pole, while in the southern hemisphere they appear to circle clockwise around the south celestial pole.

Since it lies very near the north celestial pole, Polaris, the North Star, doesn't rise and set like other stars, and appears to stay fixed in the northern sky.

CHANGING SEASONS

As Earth spins on its axis every 24 hours, it also orbits the sun over the course of a year. This means that at each stage of Earth's journey, different constellations come into view. Orion, one of the best-known constellations, is best seen on winter nights in the northern hemisphere, and during the summer months in the southern hemisphere.

Orion in the night sky

THE ZODIAC

As Earth revolves around the sun, the sun appears to drift across the stars behind it. The imaginary line that marks the sun's journey is called the ecliptic, which always stays within a band of the sky called the zodiac. The moon and the planets also follow paths through the zodiac.

Ophiuchus constellation

TWELVE SIGNS

During the course of a year, the sun passes through the 13 constellations of the zodiac. Twelve of these constellations make up the 12 signs of Western astrology. The constellation Ophiuchus (shown right) is not included in the astrological signs.

THE SUN'S JOURNEY THROUGH THE ZODIAC

Aries—the ram	April 19–May 13
Taurus—the bull	May 14–June 19
Gemini—the twins	June 20–July 20
Cancer—the crab	July 21–August 9
Leo—the lion	August 10–September 15
Virgo—the virgin	September 16– October 30
Libra—the scales	October 31–November 22
Scorpio—the scorpion	November 23–November 29
Ophiuchus—the serpent bearer	November 30–December 17
Sagittarius—the archer	December 18–January 18
Capricorn—the goat	January 19–February 15
Aquarius—the water bearer	February 16–March 11
Pisces—the fish	March 12–April 18

ASTROLOGY SIGNS

Astrologers believe that the position of the sun, stars, planets, and moon have an influence on human life. The Babylonians devised the signs of the zodiac around 3,000 years ago. However, because Earth wobbles on its axis, the North Pole is now pointing in a slightly different direction. The dates on the table above don't match the dates normally associated with the zodiac—that's because Earth's position has gradually shifted in relation to the stars.

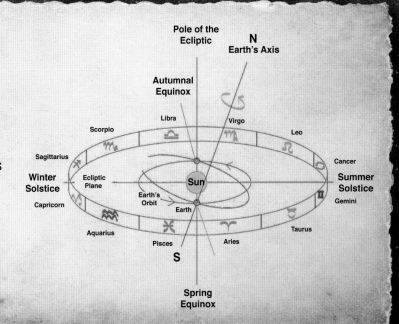

THE MILKY WAY

*T**here are countless legends that surround the Milky Way, the beautiful swath of stars that streaks across the night sky. The name Milky Way comes from the Latin Via Lactea, which means "milky."***

For the ancient Egyptians, the Milky Way was a pool of cow's milk associated with the cow-goddess Bat, while the Maya people saw it as the road along which dead souls journeyed to the underworld. In Aboriginal legends from Australia, the Milky Way is a great sky river called Wodliparri—the dark patches were believed to mark lagoons where monsters called yura were hiding.

WANDERING STARS

Thousands of years ago, ancient civilizations noticed that not all of the stars behaved in the same way. While most followed the same arc, from east to west, a few bright stars appeared to follow their own path. We now know these objects are in fact planets, but the Greeks called them "wandering stars."

FIVE PLANETS

Since Uranus and Neptune are too far away to be seen with the naked eye, early astronomers were aware of only five planets—Mercury, Venus, Mars, Jupiter, and Saturn. It was not until the eighteenth and nineteenth centuries that Neptune and Uranus were discovered. Apart from Earth, all of the planets are named after Roman gods and goddesses.

Sun

Venus

Mars

Saturn

Neptune

Mercury

Earth

Jupiter

Uranus

The cold, dark dwarf planet called Pluto was discovered in 1930. It was named after the Roman god of the underworld.

ROMAN MYTHS

Mercury was the swift god of trade and travel, and the planet was named for the speed at which it travels across the night sky. Venus, the brightest object in the sky after the sun and moon, was named after the goddess of love and beauty. Mars (shown right) was the god of war, and the planet was named for its reddish glow. Jupiter, the king of gods, lends his name to the largest planet in the solar system, while Saturn was the god of agriculture.

GOD OF DESTRUCTION

As the brightest of all the planets, Venus was given special importance by many cultures. The Sumerians worshiped the planet as the goddess Ianna, who dominated the sky and could bring death and destruction. For the Aztecs, the planet was a god called Tlahuizcalpantecuhtli. He was one of the four gods that held up the sky, and it was believed that his dazzling light could bring sickness and bad fortune.

The goddess Ianna

MYSTERIOUS MOON

With its constantly changing shape, the moon has always inspired a sense of wonder and awe. The brightest object in the night sky, the moon has been shrouded in mystery and legend for thousands of years.

THE JADE RABBIT

Many cultures have seen the shape of a rabbit in the moon's markings. One Chinese myth tells of three forest animals—a fox, a monkey, and a rabbit—that came across the Jade Emperor disguised as a starving beggar. All three animals went off to look for food for the man. The rabbit was unable to find any, and so decided to offer himself as a meal by jumping into a fire that the man had started. As a reward for his great sacrifice, the emperor carried the rabbit up to the moon to become the immortal Jade Rabbit.

The immortal Jade Rabbit

ETERNAL CHASE

The moon's ever-changing appearance over its monthly cycle—called "waxing and waning"—is a feature of many myths. The Inuit people of Greenland call their moon god Anningan. They believe he constantly chased his sister, the sun goddess Malina, across the sky, forgetting to eat and becoming thinner and thinner. Each month, he disappeared for three days—the period of the new moon—to satisfy his hunger, before returning to resume the chase.

Waxing and waning moons

Across the ages, the full moon has been associated with strange behavior in humans. In fact, the word "lunacy," meaning madness, comes from the name for the Roman goddess of the moon, Luna.

THE WOLF MOON

The Algonquin tribes of North America have many different names for the full moon, depending on the month. January's moon—when hungry wolf packs howl at night—is called the Wolf Moon, while June's moon, when fruit ripens, is called the Strawberry Moon.

SILVER MOON CHARIOT

*I*n ancient Greek myth, Selene was the name of the bewitching goddess of the moon. Her brother was Helios, the god of the sun, and her sister Eos was the goddess of the dawn. Selene fell in love with a mortal shepherd called Endymion, and since she could not bear the thought of his death, cast him into a state of eternal slumber. Each night, the goddess crossed the sky in her silver chariot, traveling down from the heavens to visit him.

AQUILA

Positioned along the eastern side of the Milky Way lie the stars of Aquila. The ancient Greeks associated this beautiful constellation with the majestic eagle. For the Romans, the constellation represented a vulture, while in Hindu religion the stars are associated with the god Vishnu.

KING OF THE BIRDS

In Greek myth, the eagle Aquila was Zeus's constant companion and carried the god's thunderbolts. On one occasion, Zeus ordered Aquila to find a handsome young man. Aquila picked out Ganymede, the son of the King of Troy. While the youth was tending sheep on a hillside, the eagle swept down and carried him off to Mount Olympus where he became a water-bearer and servant of the gods. Zeus was so pleased with Aquila that he eventually placed the bird amongst the stars.

Altair

The name of Aquila's brightest star, Altair, comes from an Arabic phrase meaning "the flying eagle."

STARRY FOOTPRINTS

In Hindu religion, Vishnu is the great protector and preserver of the universe. For the Hindus, the bright star of Altair, along with Aquila's other stars, represents the footprints of Vishnu as he strode across the heavens.

Name: Aquila—the eagle
Brightest star: Altair, nearly 17 light-years away

THE RAM &
THE GOLDEN FLEECE

Many different cultures have associated the faint constellation of Aries with a ram. For the ancient Greeks, it was connected to the dramatic tale of the winged ram and its magical fleece.

A MURDER PLOT

King Athamas ruled over a kingdom called Boeotia. Unhappily married to Nephele, he took a second wife called Ino. However, Ino was extremely jealous of the king's twin children, Phrixus and Helle. There had been no rain for months and the country's crops were failing. The cunning Ino persuaded her husband that famine could only be avoided if Phrixus and Helle were sacrificed to the gods.

MAGICAL RAM

When Nephele heard of the terrible danger facing her children, she begged the gods to save them. As Athamas prepared to kill the twins, Zeus sent a magnificent winged ram and they escaped on its back. However, as the creature flew through the night toward the kingdom of Colchis, Helle slipped from its back and plunged into the sea. The stretch of sea where she drowned is named after her: Hellespont.

THE GOLDEN FLEECE

After Phrixus arrived safely in Colchis, he sacrificed the ram to Zeus and presented its magical fleece to King Aeëtes. The king hung the fleece from a sacred tree where it was guarded day and night by a ferocious dragon that never slept. Phrixus went on to marry the king's daughter and remained in exile for the rest of his life. However, the golden fleece was eventually stolen by the hero, Jason.

CANIS MAJOR

For the ancient Greeks, the constellations Canis Major and Canis Minor represented the two dogs of the hunter Orion, faithfully following their master across the sky. Canis Major, the larger dog, contains the night sky's brightest star, Sirius—which is also known as the "dog star."

NEVERENDING CHASE

Greek myths also tell of Laelaps, a hunting hound so swift that no creature could ever outrun it. In one story, the dog was sent to catch the Teumessian fox—a gigantic beast that was so fast, it could never be caught. When news reached Zeus of these two animals trapped in an eternal hunt, he turned them both into stone and set them amongst the stars as Canis Major and Canis Minor.

The Teumessian fox

Name: Canis Major—the greater dog
Brightest star: Sirius, 8.7 light-years away

Sirius

DOG DAYS

For the ancient Egyptians, the appearance of Sirius in the night sky just before the annual flooding of the Nile was a divine symbol. The hot days of July and August followed, which is where the phrase "the dog days of summer" comes from. In Chinese culture, Sirius is known as a "heavenly wolf," while native American tribes call it the "wolf star."

Sirius, the brightest star in the sky, is over 20 times brighter than Earth's sun and twice as big. While the naked eye sees it as a single star, it is actually a "binary star" composed of two stars, Sirius A and Sirius B.

The Great Pyramids in ancient Egypt

CYGNUS

With its bright stars forming a cross (the Northern Cross), Cygnus is one of the most easily recognized constellations. For the ancient Greeks, Cygnus was a swan flying along the edge of the Milky Way. However, earlier legends associated this pattern of stars with the gigantic mythical bird known as the Roc.

Name: Cygnus—the swan
Brightest star: Deneb, thousands of light-years away

THE MIGHTY ROC

In Middle Eastern myths, the Roc was a bird of prey so enormous that it could seize an elephant in its talons. During the second voyage of Sindbad the sailor—from the Arabic tales called *The Thousand and One Nights*—Sindbad came across a gigantic Roc egg on a deserted island. When the parent Roc appeared, Sindbad tied himself to the bird's talon and was flown to a treacherous valley filled with diamonds and writhing snakes. Eventually Sindbad managed to escape the snake pit, taking with him a precious booty of treasure.

Deneb

LEDA AND THE SWAN

In one Greek myth, Zeus became besotted with Leda, the married queen of Sparta. Transforming himself into a magnificent swan, he pretended he was being pursued by an eagle so he could fly into Leda's arms for protection (shown below). Leda later produced two eggs. The twin brothers Castor and Pollux (associated with the Gemini constellation) emerged from one egg, while the twin sisters Clytemnestra and Helen of Troy came from the other. Zeus celebrated the births by placing the swan amongst the stars.

The luminous star Deneb (from the Arabic word for "tail") is the most distant bright star in the Milky Way—though its exact distance is uncertain. Together with Altair and Vega (from the constellations Aquila and Lyra), it forms part of the Summer Triangle.

LEO

One of the 12 constellations of the zodiac, Leo takes the form of a lion, its head and mane marked out by a star cluster known as the "Sickle." Leo represents the Nemean Lion killed by the Greek hero Heracles in his 12 Labors, or tasks, but is also associated with the Babylonian tale of Pyramus and Thisbe.

Name: Leo—the lion

Brightest star: Regulus, 79 light-years away

FORBIDDEN LOVE

Pyramus and Thisbe were deeply in love with each other, but their parents forbade them from seeing each other. The two communicated through a crack in the wall between their houses, and one evening arranged to meet at the edge of a forest. Arriving first, Thisbe came across a lion gnawing a dead ox. Terrified, she ran off to warn Pyramus. As she passed near the lion, her veil fluttered to the ground and was stained with the ox's blood.

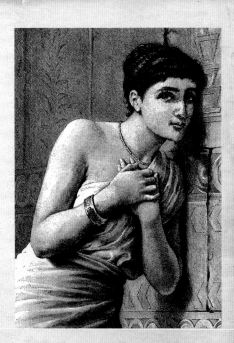

Regulus

Humbaba

BLOOD-RED BERRIES

On finishing its meal, the lion wandered away. When Pyramus arrived at the meeting place, he recognized Thisbe's bloodied veil. Believing she must be dead, he cried out in anguish and fell upon his sword. When Thisbe returned to find his dead body, she too seized the sword and killed herself. As the ground beneath the dead lovers turned red, the roots of a mulberry tree drank their blood. To this day, the fruit of all mulberry trees are stained red.

31

HIDEOUS HUMBABA

Leo has also been associated with Humbaba, an ancient monster from Sumer (modern-day Iraq and Kuwait) that guarded a sacred cedar grove. This giant is sometimes shown with claws, fangs, and the mane of a lion.

TAURUS

Taurus is the second constellation of the zodiac and one of the most impressive sights of the night sky. It contains the famous clusters called the Pleiades, or the Seven Sisters, and the Hyades. One of the oldest constellations, Taurus has been identified as a bull or cow worldwide.

Aldebaran

EUROPA AND THE BULL

In Greek myth, Zeus transformed himself into a handsome white bull in order to trick a beautiful Phoenician princess called Europa. She was playing on a beach when the gentle bull appeared. Delighted, she stroked his flanks and placed flowers around his horns before climbing onto his back. The bull carried his prize into the waves and swam across the sea to Crete. Europa later bore Zeus three sons, including the future King Minos.

Europa on the the bull's back

Pleiades

BULL'S EYE

Taurus's brightest star, Aldebaran, is thought to form the bull's fiery eye. It is a massive red giant star, 44 times as wide as our sun. In Arabic, the name means "follower," as the star seems to follow the Pleiades star cluster.

THE SEVEN SISTERS

For the Greeks, the Pleiades star cluster represented the seven daughters of Atlas, the mighty Titan who held up Earth. Native American myths tell of how the stars represent seven children who wandered amongst the stars and lost their way. One of the stars is hard to see with the naked eye; according to the myth, this is because one of the children cries so much that her tears dim her sparkling eyes.

Name: Taurus—the bull
Brightest star: Aldebaran, 65 light-years away

URSA MAJOR

Over thousands of years, many cultures have seen Ursa Major as a great bear. This constellation is the third largest in the night sky, and can be easily identified by a cluster of seven bright stars, which are often referred to as the "Big Dipper" or the "Plow."

Alioth

TURNED INTO A BEAR

In Greek myth, Zeus, the king of gods, fell in love with a nymph called Callisto. One morning, he was walking with her when he saw his wife, Hera, coming towards them. Knowing Hera's jealous nature, Zeus quickly changed Callisto into a bear. Unfortunately, Callisto's son, Arcas, was out hunting and fired an arrow at the bear. When the dying beast turned back into his mother, he was overcome with grief. Worried that Hera might find out, Zeus placed both Callisto and Arcas in the sky as the constellations Ursa Major and Ursa Minor.

Callisto and Arcas

Ursa Major contains many "deep-sky objects," such as Bode's Galaxy—which contains an astonishing 250 billion stars.

Vikings and Polaris

THE NORTH STAR

Polaris is the brightest star in Ursa Minor. Its position—almost directly above the North Pole—means sailors have long used it to navigate at sea. In Viking myths, the North Star was the glittering jewel on the end of a stake that the gods hammered through the center of the universe. Arab myths told of how Polaris was an evil star cast out to the farthest reaches of the northern sky.

Name: *Ursa Major—the great bear*

Brightest star: *Alioth, 80 light-years away*

HUNTERS & THE BEAR

In Native American myth, the four stars that form the handle of the "Big Dipper" are in fact four brave hunters eternally pursuing a great bear across the sky.

MAGICAL BEAR

There were once four brothers famed for their skill as hunters. Word reached them of a gigantic bear that was terrorizing a village. People feared it must have magical powers because although the creature left tracks, they disappeared as soon as anyone tried to follow them.

INVISIBLE TRACKS

Taking their faithful dog, the brothers set out to slay the bear. They found its giant scratch marks on a tree trunk but, as soon as the men began to follow its tracks, they vanished. Their dog, however, picked up the creature's scent. Eventually, the brothers caught sight of an enormous bear ahead of them. It began to run—but although it was swifter than a deer, the four were able to keep pace with it.

Traditional Native American arrow

ENDLESS CHASE

The pursuit went on all day. As the hunters reached the top of a mountain, darkness began to fall. The little dog yapped at the bear's heels and one of the men was able to thrust his spear into its heart. As the four stood congratulating each other, one suddenly exclaimed, "Look down!"

Far below them and all around were thousands of tiny sparkling lights. The brothers realized the chase had carried them all the way up to the stars. As they stared in amazement, the bear stirred and rose to its feet— and once again, the hunters began to pursue it across the heavens.

DRACO

Taking the form of a dragon, this sprawling constellation winds its way around the bears of Ursa Major and Ursa Minor. Draco is associated with several dragons in Greek myths, but has also been seen as a monstrous snake or, in ancient India, a crocodile.

Athena, goddess of wisdom

FROZEN IN THE STARS

One Greek tale tells of how a fearsome dragon fought with the Titans in the epic 10-year war between the old generation of Titan gods and the younger Olympian gods. As the battle raged, Athena, the Olympian goddess of wisdom, seized the dragon by its tail and hurled it high into the heavens. As it soared upwards, its long body became twisted and tied up in knots. When it neared the northern celestial pole—the point in the sky directly above the North Pole—it became frozen in the sky as the constellation Draco.

SHIFTING STAR

Today's northern pole star is Polaris, but that wasn't always the case. Around 5,000 years ago, when the ancient Egyptians were building the Pyramids, Draco's brightest star, Thuban, was the North Star. This is because over a 40,000-year cycle, the tilt of Earth's axis varies very slightly. In around 21,000 years from now, Thuban will once again be the North Star.

Thuban

Name: Draco—the Dragon
Brightest star: Thuban, 303 light-years away

Draco is a "circumpolar constellation," meaning it never sets below the horizon and is visible all year round in the northern hemisphere.

Alphard

HYDRA

Stretching across the entire night sky is Hydra, the water snake. Despite being the largest of all the constellations, it contains very few luminous stars. The brightest, Alphard, takes its name from the Arabic for "the lonely one."

The Greek hero Heracles slayed the Hydra, a many-headed water serpent, in his second labor, or task. For every head Heracles chopped off, two more grew in its place. Eventually, the hero asked his companion to hold a flame to each wound, thus preventing the heads from growing back.

ORION

With its brilliant stars that can be seen throughout the world, Orion is one of the most beautiful constellations. In Greek myths, Orion was a mighty hunter. He and his hunting dogs, represented by Canis Major and Canis Minor, are often shown as pursuing a hare—the constellation Lepus.

ORION AND SCORPIUS

Orion was the giant son of the Greek sea god, Poseidon. Handsome and incredibly strong, he was so tall he could wade through deep water. When he boasted he was capable of killing every creature on Earth, the Earth goddess Gaia sent a scorpion to sting him to death. Both Orion and the scorpion were placed amongst the stars, although these two constellations are never seen at the same time. As Orion sets in the west, Scorpius rises in the east—as if following the hunter.

BLAZING CLOUD

Orion is home to one of the loveliest sights in the night sky, the Orion Nebula. The middle "star" of Orion's sword is not actually a single star at all, but a blazing gas cloud where vast numbers of new stars are being born. It is one of the closest areas of star formation to Earth.

Orion's brightest star, Rigel, is 40,000 times brighter than Earth's sun.

Rigel

Name: *Orion—the hunter*

Brightest star: *Rigel, 864 light-years away*

ORION'S BELT AND SWORD

Many cultures have imagined Orion as a man wearing a tunic, his belt represented by a row of three bright stars and his sword a line of three fainter stars. However, for the Chimu Indians of Peru, the middle star of the "belt" represented a thief being restrained by the two stars on either side. For the Masai tribe of Kenya, the three belt stars are three old men being pursued by three lonesome widows.

CASSIOPEIA

One of the most distinctive constellations, Cassiopeia is easily recognized by its "W" or "M" shape made up of five bright stars. In Greek myths, Cassiopeia was a beautiful Ethiopian queen whose vanity led to her downfall. For the Chinese, this constellation represents a great chariot, while the Sami people of northern Europe see the antlers of a moose amongst its stars.

THE VAIN QUEEN

King Cepheus of Ethiopia and his beautiful wife, Queen Cassiopeia, had a daughter called Andromeda. Cassiopeia boasted that she and Andromeda were even lovelier than the Nereids, the nymphs of the sea. When the sea god, Poseidon, heard of the queen's vanity, he summoned a dreadful sea serpent called Cetus to plague the coast of Ethiopia. Appealing to the gods, Cepheus learned that his rule could only be saved if his daughter was sacrificed to the monster—and so Andromeda was chained to a rock and left to her fate.

The Cetus monster

Schedar

UPSIDE-DOWN

Andromeda was rescued by the hero Perseus. This enraged Poseidon, and so he decided to punish Cassiopeia by casting her into the heavens. Sitting regally on her throne, she circles the north celestial pole —though for half the year she must suffer the indignity of hanging upside-down.

EXPLODING STAR

In 1572, the famous astronomer Tycho Brahe was looking up at the night sky when he was astonished to see a brilliant new star in Cassiopeia. At the time, the universe was believed to be unchanging and so the appearance of this star—which remained visible to the naked eye for two years—stunned astronomers. We now know that it was in fact a supernova: the massive explosion of a dying star.

Name: Cassiopeia—the queen
Brightest star: Schedar, 228 light-years away

ANDROMEDA

Andromeda's four brightest stars form a line that can be easily seen on a clear night. An Ethiopian princess who was shackled to a rock by her father, Andromeda plays a key role in the stories of the nearby constellations Cassiopeia, Cepheus, Cetus, and Perseus.

PERSEUS AND PEGASUS

The hero Perseus was flying along the African coast on his winged horse, Pegasus, when he spotted King Cepheus chaining his daughter to a rock. Perseus had just slain Medusa, a snake-haired monster that could turn anything to stone, and was brimming with confidence. On discovering that Andromeda was to be sacrificed to the monster Cetus, Perseus offered to save her—on condition that they could be married.

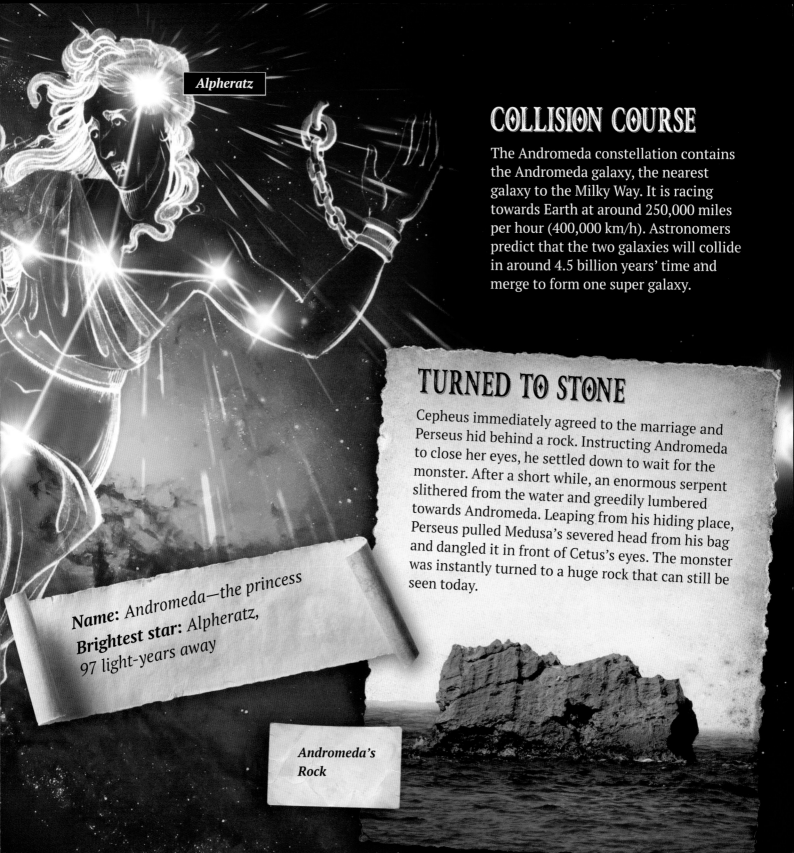

Alpheratz

COLLISION COURSE

The Andromeda constellation contains the Andromeda galaxy, the nearest galaxy to the Milky Way. It is racing towards Earth at around 250,000 miles per hour (400,000 km/h). Astronomers predict that the two galaxies will collide in around 4.5 billion years' time and merge to form one super galaxy.

TURNED TO STONE

Cepheus immediately agreed to the marriage and Perseus hid behind a rock. Instructing Andromeda to close her eyes, he settled down to wait for the monster. After a short while, an enormous serpent slithered from the water and greedily lumbered towards Andromeda. Leaping from his hiding place, Perseus pulled Medusa's severed head from his bag and dangled it in front of Cetus's eyes. The monster was instantly turned to a huge rock that can still be seen today.

Name: Andromeda—the princess
Brightest star: Alpheratz, 97 light-years away

Andromeda's Rock

HERCULES

*T*he dim, scattered stars of Hercules form the fifth-largest
constellation in the night sky. The stories of Hercules are
associated with Leo the lion, Hydra the water serpent, and Draco
the dragon.

*Brave and incredibly strong, Hercules—the Roman version of the Greek
name Heracles—was the half-mortal son of Zeus. As punishment for
a crime, he was set 12 "impossible" tasks called "labors" to carry out.
These included slaying the Nemean lion and fetching the golden apples
of Hesperides, which were guarded by the serpent Ladon.*

PERSEUS

Named after the legendary monster-slayer Perseus, this constellation is easily visible due to the brightness of its stars. It is known for the beautiful Perseid meteor shower, which occurs every August.

Name: Perseus—the hero
Brightest star: Mirfak, 590 light-years away

THE BIRTH OF A HERO

In Greek legend, Princess Danae was the daughter of King Acrisius. An oracle warned Acrisius that Danae's son would one day murder him, and so he imprisoned his daughter in a tower to prevent her from meeting any men and having children. Taking pity on Danae, the god Zeus appeared to her as a shower of gold—and nine months later, she gave birth to Perseus. When Acrisius found out, he locked mother and baby in a wooden chest and cast them out to sea. However, the pair survived and were washed ashore on the island Seriphos.

Mirfak

Algol

THE DEMON SKY

Algol is one of the best-known stars in the sky. Said to be the winking eye of snake-haired Medusa killed by Perseus, it takes its name from the Arabic for "demon's head." It is a "variable" star that brightens and dims with clockwork regularity over a cycle lasting 2 days, 20 hours and 49 minutes.

FIERY TEARS

The spectacular Perseid meteor shower occurs each year when Earth passes through a cloud of debris left behind by the comet Tuttle-Swift. In early Europe, the streaking meteors were called the "Tears of St Lawrence" in honor of Saint Lawrence, a Christian martyr who was burned to death by the Romans in 258 AD.

SLAYING THE MEDUSA

The hero Perseus is best known for killing the gorgon Medusa. He is depicted in the night sky with a sword in one hand and the monster's gruesome head in the other.

KING POLYDECTES

On the island of Seriphos, King Polydectes fell in love with Perseus's mother, Danae. However, the king was deeply unpopular and Perseus did everything he could to protect his mother from his attentions. Plotting to get rid of Perseus, Polydectes decided to hold a great banquet. His guests brought expensive gifts but Perseus arrived empty-handed. When the king challenged him, Perseus foolishly promised to bring him anything he desired. However, he had not counted on the king's answer: "Then bring me the head of Medusa!"

An ancient Greek Medusa coin

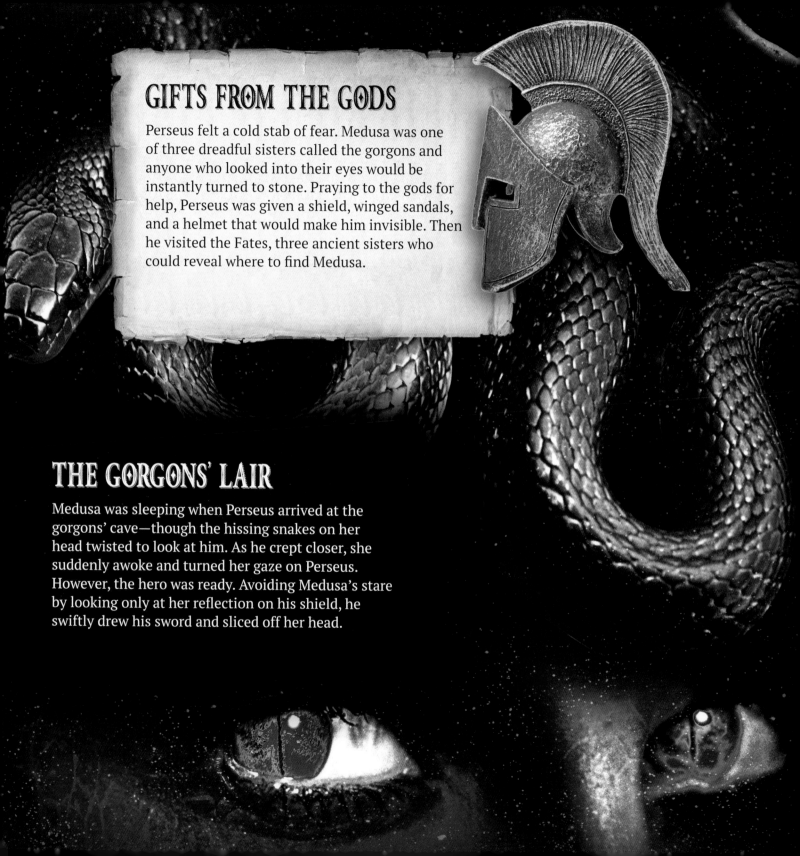

GIFTS FROM THE GODS

Perseus felt a cold stab of fear. Medusa was one of three dreadful sisters called the gorgons and anyone who looked into their eyes would be instantly turned to stone. Praying to the gods for help, Perseus was given a shield, winged sandals, and a helmet that would make him invisible. Then he visited the Fates, three ancient sisters who could reveal where to find Medusa.

THE GORGONS' LAIR

Medusa was sleeping when Perseus arrived at the gorgons' cave—though the hissing snakes on her head twisted to look at him. As he crept closer, she suddenly awoke and turned her gaze on Perseus. However, the hero was ready. Avoiding Medusa's stare by looking only at her reflection on his shield, he swiftly drew his sword and sliced off her head.

AQUARIUS

One of the 12 constellations of the zodiac, the dim stars of Aquarius can be hard to trace. Usually depicted as a man spilling water from a jar, Aquarius is situated in a part of the sky called the "the sea" because it is home to other constellations connected with water—including Pisces, the fish, and Cetus, the sea monster.

Sadalsuud

FLOODING THE NILE

In ancient Egypt, the constellation represented Hapi, the god of the Nile, and was a symbol of life. The passing of the sun in front of the stars of Aquarius would signal the start of the rainy season. The Egyptians believed that when Aquarius poured water into the Nile, the river would flood and bring fertility to the dry land.

Hapi, god of the Nile

Name: Aquarius—the water bearer
Brightest star: Sadalsuud, 540 light-years away

For the Egyptians, the rising of Sadalsuud signified the coming of spring. The name comes from an Arabic expression meaning "luck of lucks."

GLORIFIED IN THE STARS

In Greek myths, Aquarius depicts Ganymede, the handsome shepherd boy carried off by Zeus's eagle, Aquila, to be a cup bearer for the Olympian gods. Zeus's wife, Hera, was greatly angered by Ganymede's appearance because up until that point, her daughter Hebe—the goddess of youth—had filled this honored role. Furious at Hera's jealousy, Zeus celebrated Ganymede by placing him amongst the stars.

Ganymede with Aquila the eagle

THE "EYE OF GOD"

Aquarius contains the Helix Nebula, sometimes called the "eye of God"—one of the closest planetary nebulae to Earth. A planetary nebula forms when an aging star runs out of fuel, blowing its atmosphere into space and creating a colorful cloud of gas.

CENTAURUS

*L*ike the constellation Sagittarius, this dazzling pattern of stars in the southern sky takes the form of a centaur—a creature with the head, arms, and chest of a man, and the body of a horse.

In Greek myths, Chiron was a gifted teacher who was known for his skills in everything from hunting and archery to medicine and music. Wise, noble, and intelligent, Chiron was very different from his fellow centaurs, who often displayed wild and savage behavior.

CRUX

Despite being the smallest of the 88 constellations, the four brightest main stars of Crux, or the Southern Cross, make it one of the most famous sights of the southern night sky. It holds particular importance in Australia and New Zealand, where it can be seen all year round.

Acrux

VANISHING STARS

The ancient Greeks viewed Crux as part of the constellation Centaurus. However, due to the changing tilt of Earth's axis over thousands of years, its stars gradually disappeared below the horizon for most of the northern hemisphere. It was not until the sixteenth century that European explorers, on their voyages to the southern hemisphere, rediscovered its brilliant stars.

Name: Crux—the cross
Brightest star: Acrux,
323 light-years away

LEGENDS OF THE CROSS

For the Incas, the stars of Crux represented the center of the universe. The cross symbolized the three levels of the world: the heavens, the world of the living, and the underworld, inhabited by the spirits of the dead. For some Aboriginal tribes of Australia, Crux, together with a dark patch of sky called the Coalsack Nebula, is the "Emu in the Sky." The Aboriginal Australians see emus as spirits of creation that flew across the land.

THE GREAT SKY CANOE

In New Zealand, the Maori people have several different legends surrounding Crux. One group sees it as an anchor, called Te Punga, of a giant sky canoe. For another group, it is a hole in the sky through which storm winds escaped.

An Inca cross

CARINA

The southern stars of Carina used to be part of a much larger constellation, Argo Navis, which was named after the famous *Argo* ship of Greek myths. In the eighteenth century, Argo Navis was divided into three smaller constellations: Carina (the keel), Puppis (the stern), and Vela (the sails).

Canopus

Carina contains the night sky's second brightest star, Canopus. It is easily visible from the southern hemisphere for much of the year.

THE HERO JASON

The great Greek hero Jason was a baby when his father, the king of Iolcos, was overthrown by his brother Pelias. When Jason grew up, he returned to Iolcos to reclaim the kingdom. Pelias told him he would only give up the throne if Jason fetched the Golden Fleece, the magical pelt of a winged ram, from Colchis. He was sure Jason could never succeed for the fleece was guarded by a dragon that never slept.

STAR BOAT

When the Argonauts finally arrived in Colchis, Jason faced many more challenges before he was able to outwit the dragon and seize the Golden Fleece. He later dedicated the *Argo* to the sea god Poseidon—who placed it amongst the stars.

THE ARGONAUTS

Jason built a magnificent ship, the *Argo*, and gathered together a band of heroes called the Argonauts. Amongst their number were Heracles, and Kalais and Zetes, the winged twin sons of Boreas (the north wind). On their way to Colchis, the Argonauts had many thrilling adventures. These included facing the winged Harpies, terrifying creatures with women's faces and vultures' bodies, and being attacked by savage giants.

PEGASUS

*T*his northern constellation representing a winged horse is one of the largest in the night sky. Its companion is Equuleus, the foal, which is the second smallest constellation.

In Greek myths, Pegasus was a magnificent winged stallion. His father was Poseidon, the god of the sea, and his mother was the Gorgon Medusa. Pegasus carried the hero Bellarophon across the sky on his quest to slay the fire-breathing monster, called the Chimera.

GEMINI

The zodiac constellation of Gemini is a beautiful sight in northern winter skies. Its two brightest stars, Castor and Pollux, are named after twin brothers in Greek myths. These starry "twins" have also been associated with the legendary founders of Rome, Romulus and Remus.

Castor

Pollux

Name: Gemini—the twins
Brightest star: Castor,
51 light-years away

INSEPARABLE TWINS

In Greek myths, the twin brothers Castor and Pollux shared the same mother, Leda, but had different fathers. As the son of the god Zeus, Pollux was immortal, while Castor, the son of Leda's husband, was mortal. The two brothers did everything together, such as joining the hero Jason on his quest to find the Golden Fleece. When Castor died, the immortal Pollux was sick with grief. To console him, Zeus fixed both brothers in the sky as the stars of Gemini.

THE GEMINIDS

Each year around December 13–14, a spectacular meteor shower, called the Geminids, appears to radiate from near the star Castor. At the peak of the display, up to 100 meteors can be seen in a single hour.

ST ELMO'S FIRE

Sailors have long reported seeing a strange, sudden glow of light on the masts of their ships, often just before or after a storm. Scientists now understand what causes this electrical weather phenomenon—called St Elmo's Fire—but for the ancient Greeks, the fiery light was a signal that Castor and Pollux were protecting them during a storm.

65

LYRA

Lying on the western edge of the Milky Way, this impressive constellation represents the lyre—a stringed musical instrument popular in ancient Greece. It contains Vega, the fifth brightest star in the heavens.

Vega

JOURNEY TO THE UNDERWORLD

In Greek myths, Lyra is associated with the musician Orpheus. His music was so beautiful, that even animals were charmed by it. When his beloved wife, Eurydice, died of a snakebite, Orpheus vowed that he would journey deep into the underworld to fetch her back.

Arab astronomers saw the shape of an eagle in Lyra's stars. Its brilliant star, Vega, takes its name from an Arabic phrase meaning "swooping eagle."

Orpheus, the musician

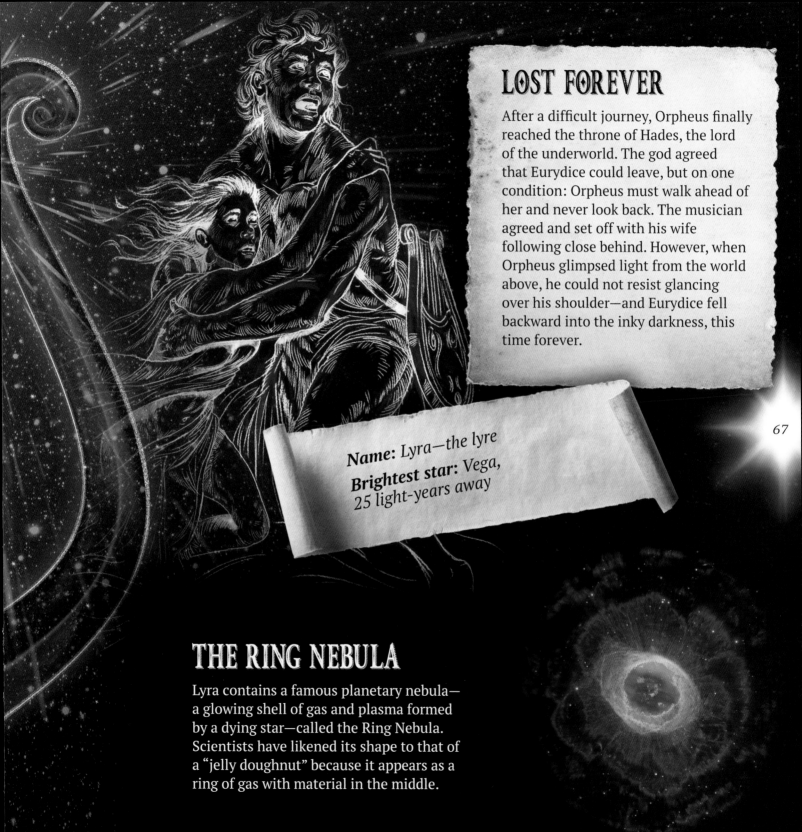

LOST FOREVER

After a difficult journey, Orpheus finally reached the throne of Hades, the lord of the underworld. The god agreed that Eurydice could leave, but on one condition: Orpheus must walk ahead of her and never look back. The musician agreed and set off with his wife following close behind. However, when Orpheus glimpsed light from the world above, he could not resist glancing over his shoulder—and Eurydice fell backward into the inky darkness, this time forever.

Name: Lyra—the lyre
Brightest star: Vega, 25 light-years away

THE RING NEBULA

Lyra contains a famous planetary nebula— a glowing shell of gas and plasma formed by a dying star—called the Ring Nebula. Scientists have likened its shape to that of a "jelly doughnut" because it appears as a ring of gas with material in the middle.

THE LEGEND OF TANABATA

Altair

On the seventh day of the seventh month—July 7—the star festival of Tanabata takes place in Japan. It celebrates the love between a princess and a cow herder, who are represented by Vega, the brightest star in Lyra, and Altair, the brightest star in Aquila.

VEGA AND ALTAIR

Princess Orihime (Vega) spent her days sitting by a great river, the Milky Way, weaving beautiful clothes. Worried that she was lonely, her father—the god of heaven—arranged for her to meet Hikoboshi (Altair), a cow herder. The two fell deeply in love and were married. However, the couple were so besotted with each other that Orihime stopped sewing and Hikoboshi allowed his cattle to wander across the heavens.

Vega

STAR-CROSSED

Orihime's father was furious, and decided to separate the pair. They were to live on opposite sides of the Milky Way, and would only be allowed to see each other once a year, on the seventh day of the seventh month.

On the day of Tanabata, the people of Japan write wishes on strips of colored paper and hang them from bamboo trees.

CROSSING THE RIVER

When the time came for the pair to be reunited, Orihime found that the Milky Way was impossible to cross. However, a flock of magpies took pity on the weeping princess and made a bridge for her with their wings. Legend tells that if ever it rains on July 7 then the birds will not appear—and the pair must wait another year before they can see each other again.

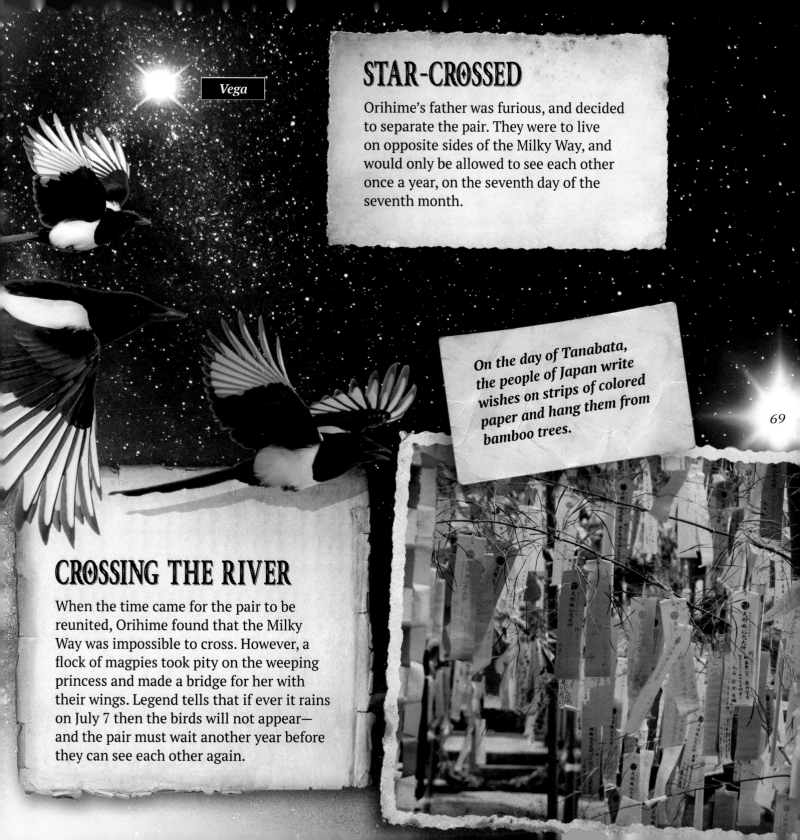

GLOSSARY

Astrology: The study of how the movement of the stars and planets have a supposed influence on our lives.

Axis: An imaginary line around which something rotates. Earth's axis passes through the North and South Poles.

Babylonians: People from Babylonia, an ancient city state in Mesopotamia (a region that is now part of Iraq).

Cedar: A large, evergreen tree.

Celestial: Positioned in the sky or space.

Circumpolar: Situated around one of Earth's poles.

Comet: An object that moves around the sun, leaving a bright trail behind it.

Constellation: A group of stars that forms an imaginary shape when viewed from Earth.

Crete: The largest of the Greek islands.

Deep-sky object: A space object outside our solar system.

Divine: Coming from or connected with a god or goddess.

Dome: A shape resembling the top half of a ball.

Equator: An imaginary line drawn around the middle of Earth, dividing it into two equal parts.

Exile: When a person is made to live away from their country.

Galaxy: A huge system of stars in the universe.

Gorgon: A monster with a deadly stare from Greek myth.

Grove: A group of trees.

Hemisphere: A half of the Earth, usually above or below the equator (northern and southern hemispheres).

Horizon: The line in the distance where Earth or the sea seems to meet the sky.

Immortal: Someone who can live forever.

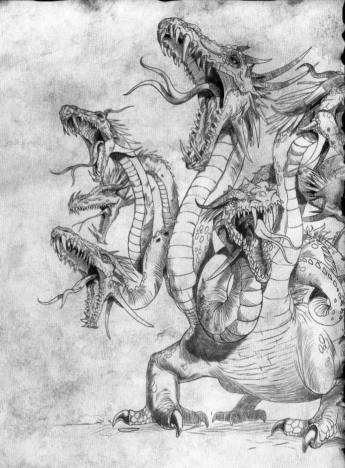

Lagoon: A shallow lake separated from the sea or a river by sand or rocks.

Martyr: A person who is killed because of their religious beliefs.

Meteor: A small space rock that produces a bright light as it travels through Earth's atmosphere.

Mortal: Unable to live forever and destined to die.

Mount Olympus: A mountain in Greece, said to be the home of the Olympian gods.

Nebula: A huge cloud of gas and dust in space.

Olympian gods: The most important ancient Greek gods.

Oracle: Someone who passes on messages said to come from the gods.

Phoenician: From Phoenicia, an ancient Mediterranean kingdom (stretching through a region that is now Lebanon, Syria, and Israel).

Plasma: A very hot gas that is common in space but rare on Earth.

Pole: Either the northernmost (North Pole) or southernmost (South Pole) place on Earth.

Red giant: A dying star in the last stages of its life cycle.

Sami people: An ethnic group living in Sweden, Norway, Finland, and Russia.

Sphere: A shape like a ball.

Star cluster: A group of stars held together by gravity.

Titan: A god from the family of ancient Greek gods that came before the Olympian gods.

Treatise: A long and serious piece of writing dealing with a particular subject.

Underworld: A place beneath Earth's surface where the spirits of the dead are said to go.

Zeus: King of the ancient Greek gods.

INDEX